Sleeping Babies

Written and illustrated
by TONY AUTH

A GOLDEN BOOK • NEW YORK
Western Publishing Company, Inc., Racine, Wisconsin 53404

Baby Katie did not want to fall asleep. She wanted to stay awake and play with Mommy and Daddy. "No one in the world has to go to sleep but me," Katie cried to Mommy.

"Oh, but that's not true, Katie," said Mommy. "Why, little babies everywhere are already fast alseep. And soon you will be, too.

"All the baby hoot owls are asleep.

"All the tiny baby mice are asleep.

"All the baby badgers are asleep.

"All the baby bees are asleep.

"All the baby whales are asleep.

"All the baby pandas are asleep.

"All the baby weasels are asleep.

"All the baby otters are asleep.

"All the baby bear cubs are asleep.

"All the baby hippos are asleep.

"All the newborn baby kittens are asleep.

"All the baby foxes are asleep.

"All the baby frogs are asleep.

"And all the little children are asleep.
"Good night!"